THE Crooked HOUSE

Anne Peterson

Illustrations by Jessica Peterson

This book is dedicated to anyone who has ever felt *crooked.*

Long ago, in a town by the river, there once was a beautiful place.
With rows of nice houses, so pretty to see, and a smile upon everyone's face.

All except for one house that was crooked, for inside lived a girl who was sad.
Kerrie never invited her friends to come see, the house she was sorry she had.

Kerrie looked at the rooms all around her. They were cozy and looked rather fine.
But the fact that her house was so crooked—well it bothered her all of the time.

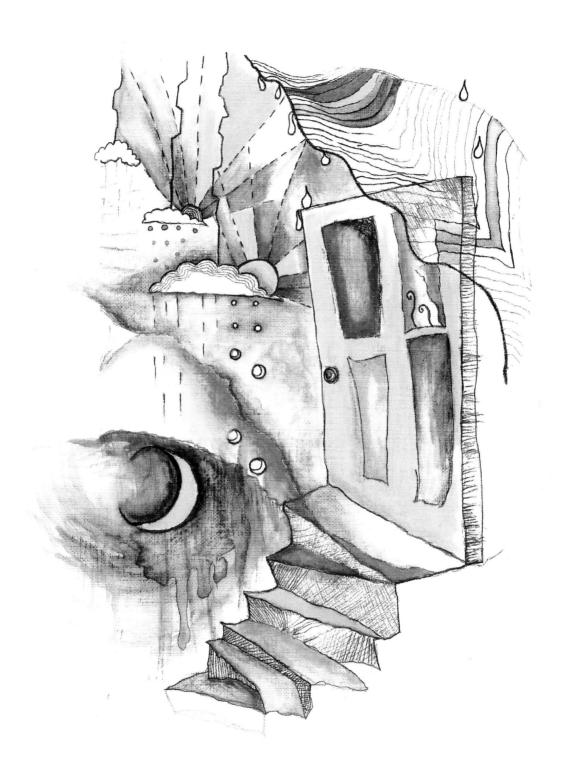

Every evening when Kerrie was sleeping, she would picture her house in her dreams.
There were colors and rainbows all over the place, but her house was still crooked, it seems.

Then one day, little Kerrie went walking, she saw people her mom and dad knew.
And they smiled as they asked her, "How are you, my dear?"
And she answered,"I'm fine, how are you?"

But the woman looked closer at Kerrie. As she said, "Are you *sure* you're okay?
For to us, you look very unhappy. Can we help you with something today?"

"Both my husband and I see you walking, as you pass by our house on your way,
and we are just wondering, which house is *yours*? Do you think you can tell us today?"

Kerrie started to feel quite uneasy, and she trembled, afraid she might cry.
For she simply did not want to say where she lived, but she also did *not* want to lie.

Kerrie gulped as she thought for a moment, while she hoped that the questions were done.
And then pointing, she answered, "I live over there—my house is the yellow one."

"Oh, the small *crooked* house?" she said kindly, as Kerrie's face turned rosy red.
Then the woman reached over and touched Kerrie's arm,
"But, do you know the *story*?" she said.

Kerrie cringed when she heard the word *crooked*, even though she'd agree it was true.
She just never felt good that she lived in that house, and at times, she would feel *crooked* too.

So the old woman started her story, "Years ago, in a storm—strong winds blew.
And we all ran inside, for we wanted to hide, so uncertain of what we should do.

Then everything grew very quiet, till we heard a loud sound like a train.
And the sky turned a green, no one ever had seen.
There was wind everywhere mixed with rain.

And we suddenly saw a tornado,
as it tossed every thing everywhere.
We saw furniture, leaves—things you wouldn't believe;
and we watched them fly up in the air.

And just when we thought it was over, the tornado without any sound,
it picked up your house and it spun it around, and it set it back down on the ground.

It's so lucky your house was still empty, when the storm hit our town, on that day.
And perhaps now you see, after listening to me, why your house is so crooked today.

Kerrie listened to all of the story, and her eyes opened up very wide,
"My house was in a tornado?" she gasped. "Oh my goodness! I'm really surprised."

And then Kerrie asked in a whisper, "May I tell you a secret of mine?
I have never invited my friends to my house, for you see, I'm ashamed all the time."

The couple looked over at Kerrie. They were smiling because they both knew
that a child wants to be like the children they see; fitting in is a hard thing to do.

But suddenly Kerrie felt different, after hearing the story that day.
She no longer felt bad for the house that she had.
So she waved and went skipping away.

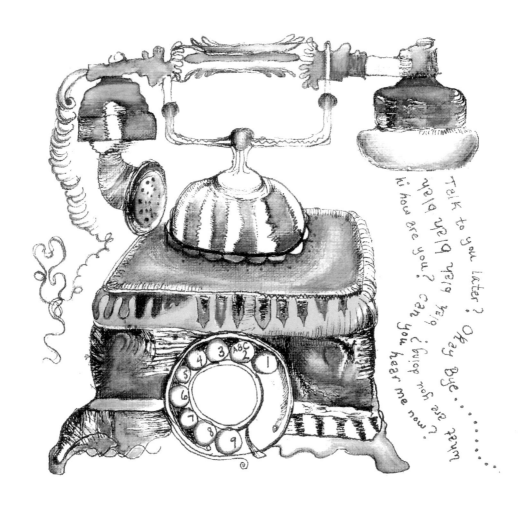

Later on, Kerrie's phone started ringing. It was Sadie who called her to say,
"My mom and dad said, you could come to our house, would you like to sleep over today?"

Kerrie found that she could not stop giggling, sleeping over was such fun to do.
But instead, what she said was surprising, that it even surprised Kerrie too.

Kerrie said, "Would *you* like to come over? We can play, we can talk, we can eat.
And she heard Sadie say, "Oh I'd *love* to come there, coming over would be such a treat!"

So then Sadie came over to Kerrie's house. And they ate, and they talked while they played.
And then Kerrie told Sadie the story she heard—how her house became crooked one day.

In a week, it would be Kerrie's birthday, and with parties there's so much to do.
She would have to send out invitations, of course, and invite all her friends to come too.

"Kerrie, what kind of cake can I make you?"
Kerrie's mom asked her daughter one day.

And then scratching her head, Kerrie smiled as she said,
"Just surprise me, it's special that way."

When everyone sang *Happy Birthday*, Kerrie smiled as she looked at her cake.
For it looked like her house that was crooked, the best cake any mother could make.

Oh, the fun Kerrie had at her party, with the house all filled up with her friends.
They all laughed as they played silly games through the day. And she hoped that it never would end.

Kerrie learned that while some things are *different,* it does not mean that different is *bad.* And she learned that her house was unique, so to speak. So no longer did Kerrie feel sad.

Long ago, in a town by the river, lived some people who often felt glad.
But especially someone named Kerrie, who was proud of the house that she had.

Anne Peterson is a poet, speaker and author of three published books. This is her second children's book. Her first was *Emma's Wish*. Anne has also written *Real Love: Guaranteed to Last*, and *BROKEN: A Story of Abuse and Survival*. You can see more of her work at www.annepeterson.com or visit her at **https://www.facebook.com/annepetersonwrites**

Jessica Peterson is a graduate from ICC with a major in Fine Art. Her first book she illustrated was *Emma's Wish*. In addition, she also did the covers for *Real Love: Guaranteed to Last,* and *BROKEN: A Story of Abuse and Survival*. You can see more of her work at www.jessicapetersonart.com or find her at **https://www.facebook.com/jessicapetersonart**

Made in the USA
Middletown, DE
25 February 2019